How the Ladies
Stopped the Wind

by **Bruce McMillan**

illustrated with paintings by **Gunnella**

Houghton Mifflin Company
Boston 2007
Walter Lorraine Books

More information about the author can be found at www.brucemcmillan.com.
More information about the illustrator can be found at www.gunnella.info.

The oil paintings were done using Winsor & Newton Winton Oil Colours and Winsor & Newton Short Flat Galleria brushes on Fredrix Standard Red Label prestretched canvas, and covered with Winsor & Newton Retouching Varnish.

Walter Lorraine *wr* Books

www.houghtonmifflinbooks.com

Library of Congress Cataloging-in-Publication Data

McMillan, Bruce.
  How the ladies stopped the wind / by Bruce McMillan; illustrated with paintings by Gunnella.
    p. cm.
  "Walter Lorraine books."
  Summary: The women of one village in Iceland decide to plant trees to stop the powerful winds that make it difficult even to go for a walk, but first they must find a ways to prevent sheep from eating all of their saplings, while encouraging chickens to fertilize them.
  ISBN-13: 978-0-618-77330-5 (hardcover)
  [1. Trees—Fiction. 2. Winds—Fiction. 3. Sheep—Fiction. 4. Chickens—Fiction. 5. Iceland—Fiction.] I. Gunnella, ill. II. Title.

  PZ7.M2278How 2007
  [E]—dc22
                                    2007004207

Manufactured in Singapore
TWP 10 9 8 7 6 5 4 3 2 1

Designed by Bruce McMillan
The text is set in 20-point Cochin.

Going for a walk can often be difficult in Iceland. It's too windy. The ladies in one village decided they should do something about this.

One solution was to lie down and let the wind blow over them.
This gave the ladies time to think of a better solution, and they did.

The ladies thought, "Let's plant some trees. They will grow tall and will surely stop the wind."

The ladies knew the chickens would help. But they thought the sheep could be a problem.

The trees arrived. The ladies planted them in the village and in the country too.

The chickens were excited. The sheep were curious. They had never seen trees before.

On calm days the ladies and their daughters sang to the sheep. The chickens sang too. They sang, "Please, please, don't eat the trees. Please, please, don't eat the trees."

The sheep had no idea what they were singing about.

The ladies thought their singing was working. The sheep were eating only grass.

The ladies fed the chickens leftover potatoes. They told the chickens, "You need to help too."

It was the chickens' job to make fertilizer for the trees. They did their job very well.

Then the sheep discovered the tasty buds on the trees. The ladies herded them away, but the sheep always came back. The sheep ate all of the tiny trees.

The ladies ordered more trees. But they wondered, "What will we do about the sheep?"

"What about the cows?" they thought. "The cows only eat grass."
So the ladies spoke to the cows. "Please herd the sheep away from
the trees. Please lead them to the grass."

Then the ladies built a fence around the village and sang, "Sheep stay out, the cows are your friends. Sheep go away, just follow your friends."

The ladies liked to sing.

The new trees arrived. The ladies planted them in the countryside, far beyond the village fences.

The young ladies helped. The curious sheep watched.

The ladies and their young helpers walked back to town.
The sheep followed until they reached the gate. The sheep
were not allowed in.

Under darkening rain clouds, the ladies planted trees all around the village.

Looking over the fence, the sheep were so curious they forgot about the trees in the country.

When all of the trees were planted, the ladies celebrated.

They made cakes and doughnuts. The sheep got bored looking through the fence. When they saw the cows, the sheep followed them to the country pastures.

The ladies' plan seemed to be working. The sheep were eating
grass with the cows.

Sometimes the chickens did too good a job making fertilizer. When that happened, the ladies were prepared. They went to check on the trees wearing more than just their shoes.

The trees were growing. The chickens were fertilizing. The ladies were content. When the friendly cows came to visit, they didn't come alone.

The sheep always followed the cows, but the fence kept them away from the trees. All was well — for now.

But just like babies, the sheep were always hungry. They didn't leave much grass for the cows. The cows were not happy with their friends.

One day the ladies
took the children to the
country for a picnic.
The curious sheep soon
arrived, but the cows
were nowhere in sight.

With no cows to keep the sheep away from the tasty trees, all the trees in the countryside were soon gone. But fortunately, the fences around the village kept the sheep out and the chickens were still making fertilizer.

Day after day, the
ladies watched the trees
in the village grow.
They were sure the trees
grew faster when they
were watching them.

But the young ladies knew better. It was the fertilizer that made the trees grow so fast and so tall. The young ladies always thanked the chickens for helping.

Over the years the
trees in the village grew
taller and taller.

The young ladies became ladies. They had babies of their own.

On their village walks they never had to worry about the wind.

High above the trees, birds soared on the wind. Down by the trees, the ladies played with their young children. Nobody blew over.

Word spread. Ladies in other villages planted trees too.

Everyone danced and sang, "Chickens please, help our trees.

Chickens please, help our trees."

It was the most popular song in all of Iceland.

In the Icelandic countryside you can still see forever. There are no trees to block the beautiful views—or the strong wind. But thanks to the ladies, there are trees in the villages to stop the wind.

Every year, seeds from the trees sprout. Young seedlings take root and more trees grow . . .

. . . except where the wind blows the fences down. Hungry sheep
never miss a tasty treat.